HAROLD

WestBow Press books may be ordered through booksellers or by contacting:

WestBow Press
A Division of Thomas Nelson & Zondervan
1663 Liberty Drive
Bloomington, IN 47403
www.westbowpress.com
1 (866) 928-1240

ISBN: 978-1-9736-3812-4 (sc)
ISBN: 978-1-9736-3813-1 (e)

Library of Congress Control Number: 2018910226

Print information available on the last page.

WestBow Press rev. date: 10/31/2018

WESTBOW
PRESS®
A DIVISION OF THOMAS NELSON
& ZONDERVAN

HAROLD

WRITTEN BY MELISSA CLARK

Illustrated by Sam Orozco

For my Heavenly Father, without whom this book would not have been created. You are my joy and my mainstay.

For my earthly father, Larry, who said, "I know your book will light up some little people's lives."
Rest with Jesus, Dad, your passion for encouraging children will live on.

and

For Evan, you never let me give up on Harold. I love you forever.

Harold was a little angel with a large problem. Each time he opened his mouth, loud LOUD music came out. Try as he might, Harold couldn't say ANY words. He'd twist his mouth this way and that, but he could only make...music. No achoos, no bless-yous. No pleases or thank yous. Just very. Loud. Music. Even the smallest crack in Harold's grin could blast the sunset off of a cloud!

The music was so beautiful! It was full of flutes and lutes. Trumpets and tambourines. Horns and harps. There were drums and gongs and chimes!! There was nothing wrong with the gorgeous music. It was just very, VERY, LOUD. And it made Harold very, *very* lonely. No one wanted to take the chance "The Sound" would blast 'em!

Harold adored Divine Chorus! The songs the other angels sang made his toes tap, but he could never sing along. Oh, how he longed to make the "O's" and "ah's" like the others. His best curl sagged with frustration.

During his "Worship 101" class, Harold was so moved by the music he forgot to keep his mouth closed. The bright and robust music blew Mr. Hymn's halo clean off of his head!

After that, Gregory Gilde and Wendy Wingling called him "Trumpet Tongue". That made Harold so sad.

Harold's parents loved him very much. They thought Harold was perfect just the way he was, even if they had to wear protective ear-ware in case Harold had to sneeze. When Harold would come home with a forlorn look on his face, they would say, "It's okay, little Angel, God has everything in hand."

He didn't know *what* that meant precisely, but Harold desperately wanted to find out.

As he sat on his favorite fluffy "thinking" cloud, Harold pondered his plight. He pondered and considered. Then, he considered and pondered. The best curl on his forehead bounced with each of his most thoughtful thoughts.

Could it be God was mad at him? Had he popped God's most fluffy cloud when he was a baby and this was the punishment? Did God make a mistake when He made Harold but decided to give him to Mom and Dad anyway? Poor Harold! He sat a whole day and two hours pondering. A tiny angel tear trickled down his tiny angel cheek.

"Why what's the matter, little angel?" said a friendly voice.

Harold looked up to see the face of the arch angel, Gabriel, himself. Harold turned a bright shade of pink as Gabriel grinned at him. Wondering what such an important angel was doing talking to him, Harold simply stared and let Gabriel continue.

"I need you to come with me to the heavenly gate, Harold."

"Great, I'm probably getting kicked out of heaven," Harold thought to himself.

As they neared heaven's gate, Harold saw all the angels of heaven gathered on clouds as far as he could see. What were they all doing there? Were they there to cheer as he got thrown out of heaven? Harold's best curl seemed to shake on his forehead as he walked with Gabriel to the front of all the angels.

"Now, little angel, it is time to open your mouth!" Gabriel told him firmly, but lovingly.

Harold knew what was going to happen and he was afraid. He shook his head quickly and clapped his hands over his mouth. His best curl trembled with utter fear!

"Please, Harold, you'll see why in a minute. You have a very important job to do today. Open your mouth."

Harold took a deep breath, closed his eyes, crossed his fingers and said a prayer. He opened his mouth as wide as it could go!! Over the clouds barreled the joyous music and when it reached the gates they burst open wide!

All the angels cheered and everyone leaped from their clouds! They flew toward the gate with Harold and Gabriel in the lead! The little angel held tightly to Gabriel's hand as they swooped down to earth, and the music blared brightly before them. It didn't sound so out of place out there in the sky, where there weren't so many clouds. Harold felt like he never felt before, it was as though he had been waiting for this his whole life!

He sang and did flippy-dips! He sang and did whirly-twirls! He sang and did floppy-drops! His best curl hung on for dear life as Harold rejoiced at his new discovery!

Down below, Harold noticed there were shepherds and their sheep looking up at all the angels in the sky. Gabriel disappeared to go talk to them and Harold continued to hang his mouth wide open while the other angels sang along with him.

All too soon, Gabriel was back and ushering everyone back to Heaven's gate. Harold didn't want to go. He wanted to sing his music forever. Reluctantly, he followed everyone home with joy in his heart, but he had questions in his mind.

Gabriel and Harold sat on a cloud with a hot cup "Strato-cider" and Gabriel explained what just happened.

"Harold, tonight was a night we angels have been waiting for, for a long time. Do you know what it is?"

Harold had no idea, but was very keen to find out all about it.

"You see, tonight a baby was born. His name is Jesus and He has been sent by God to show all the world how much God loves them. He is going to grow up and become a man who changes how people love each other. They are going to be able to know and love God differently, too. Tonight began that journey and that is why we went to earth to tell those people what they'd been waiting for was finally here. We needed your special gift to get the shepherds attention!"

The story made Harold's whole body giggle with giddiness from the top of his head to the tips of his toes. He felt a grand feeling just before he opened his mouth and let out a giant *BOOM!*

At first, the change shocked him! Then, Harold realized something. He could change the sound from his mouth with the feelings in his heart! Before, he was so afraid of the loud, LOUD music that he never tried anything but keeping it quiet. He tried a softer sound like the sound of the baby Jesus laughing. Out came a light and happy flute song! He thought of his Mom and Dad and how much he loved them. Out came a glorious harp solo! What fun!

Harold now knew without a doubt, God wasn't mad at him and God hadn't made a mistake. He'd made Harold for a special purpose on a special day. Though Harold had tried to hide his gift, he finally knew it was part of who he was, and that made him happy! Even Harold's best curl on his forehead sprang up and agreed!

From that day forward, the word *herald* means "to tell loudly of important news". That is why we sing about the "Harold" Angels, for it took a rather small angel named Harold with a LOUD sound to lead all the angels in song on that special day.

Now, Harold accompanies the choir with all his different musical sounds. And when he gets called "Trumpet Tongue" every now and then, he doesn't even mind anymore.

THE END

LET'S TALK ABOUT WHAT HAROLD LEARNED!

*Ecclesiastes 3:11- "God has made everything beautiful in its own time."(NLT)

Harold felt very alone and misunderstood and so do many others. Sometimes, it takes a while for God to show you why you look, act and feel the way you do. Just like Harold. Don't worry, He thinks you are beautiful and amazing no matter what.

Have you ever felt ugly? Have you ever felt like no one understands what you are going through or doesn't care? What happened?

*Romans 8:28 - For we know that God causes everything to work together for the good of those who love God and are called according to His purpose for them.(NLT)

Did you know you have a purpose in this world only YOU were created to have? When God created you He thought about the best time in history to place you. He thought about all the people you would ever meet and the lives you could change. He also wants to put your life together to work well for you because you love Him.

What are your talents? Do you love to draw or color? Do you love to run around really fast? Do you love to hug others and make them feel happy? Tell me about why you think God put those things in you to give you purpose.

*John 12:46- "I have come as a light to shine in this dark world, so that all who put their trust in me will no longer remain in the dark."(NLT)

Precious young person, you have an important place in this world. But even more importantly, you have a person God sent just for you to be able to rely on all the time. Even if you think no one likes you or you were really bad, he promises you can trust him. Jesus promises He will be a bright light of love and joy for you. No one else may know what you are going through, but Jesus says He does. He wants to shine a light on all parts of your life so you can notice the difference between life without Him and life with Him.

When do you feel really happy? When do you feel misunderstood?

What are some things in your life that seem like they will never change? Do you think Jesus will show you how to change them? Why?

Let's say this out loud and together. (if your child cannot read please say a few words at a time and let him or her repeat them. If he or she can read, please let him/her have time to get through it themselves).

God, I understand now, that I am made for a purpose. I have a special place in this world you designed just for me. I am not ugly to you. I am beautiful/handsome to you and to myself. I see myself how you see me, as someone irreplaceable and loved. Jesus, thank you for shining your light in the parts of my life that are tough for me or dark to me. You make them bright with your love. It may take time for me to see all of the things you see in me, but I am willing to trust you that you want the best for me in every way. Talk to you soon, amen.

Harold learned about the day Jesus was born and how Jesus was going to show the world to love one another and God differently. The most important way Jesus did that was by dying on a cross so we can be free from sin. Sin isn't just really bad things, it's little things like telling your parents no, or not wanting to share a toy. Those things separated humans from God for a long time and God wanted us back. He wanted us back so badly that he sent Jesus to earth for 33 years to teach people a new way of thinking and then to take all those bad things people do to the cross to die with him. He set us free! If you believe Jesus did that, I have good news to share with you! He can live in your heart forever and help you through life if you are willing to listen to Him. What a cool guy! You only need to say this prayer.

Dear God, I know I do naughty things sometimes and that takes me far away from you. I'm sorry for doing those things and I want to be close to you. I think Jesus died on a cross a long time ago and saved me so I could be right next to you. Jesus, please come into my heart and show me how much you love me. I want to learn from you and listen to you. From this day forward the naughty things I did are forgotten and I'm a new person! Thank you Jesus, amen.